**DO NOT REMOVE
CARDS FROM POCKET**

3/94

# Ska-tat!

## Kimberley Knutson

MACMILLAN PUBLISHING COMPANY • NEW YORK

Maxwell Macmillan Canada • Toronto

Maxwell Macmillan International • New York   Oxford   Singapore   Sydney

Macmillan Publishing Company, 866 Third Avenue, New York, NY 10022

Maxwell Macmillan Canada, Inc., 1200 Eglinton Avenue East,
Suite 200, Don Mills, Ontario M3C 3N1

Macmillan Publishing Company is part of the
Maxwell Communication Group of Companies.

First edition
Printed in the United States of America

10  9  8  7  6  5  4  3  2  1

The text of this book is set in 16 point ITC Leawood Medium.
The illustrations are rendered in handmade paper and collage.

Library of Congress Cataloging-in-Publication Data
Knutson, Kimberley.
Ska-tat! / Kimberley Knutson. — 1st. ed.
p.      cm.
Summary: Children describe playing in the colorful,
scratchy leaves as they fall down from the trees.
ISBN 0-02-750846-3
[1. Leaves—Fiction.]  I. Title.
PZ7.K7864Sk  1993
[E]—dc20      92-38072

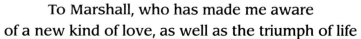

To Marshall, who has made me aware
of a new kind of love, as well as the triumph of life

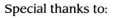

Special thanks to:

Susan and Jean for
their continued faith in me;

Ray for putting up with
all the leaves;

my family
and friends
for their glee, energy and insight;

my sweetheart
Michael
for his great solutions and constant support;

and Shoshi,
for sharing her trees.

Sh-kah sh-kah

hurrah!

The leaves are waggling

in the trees.

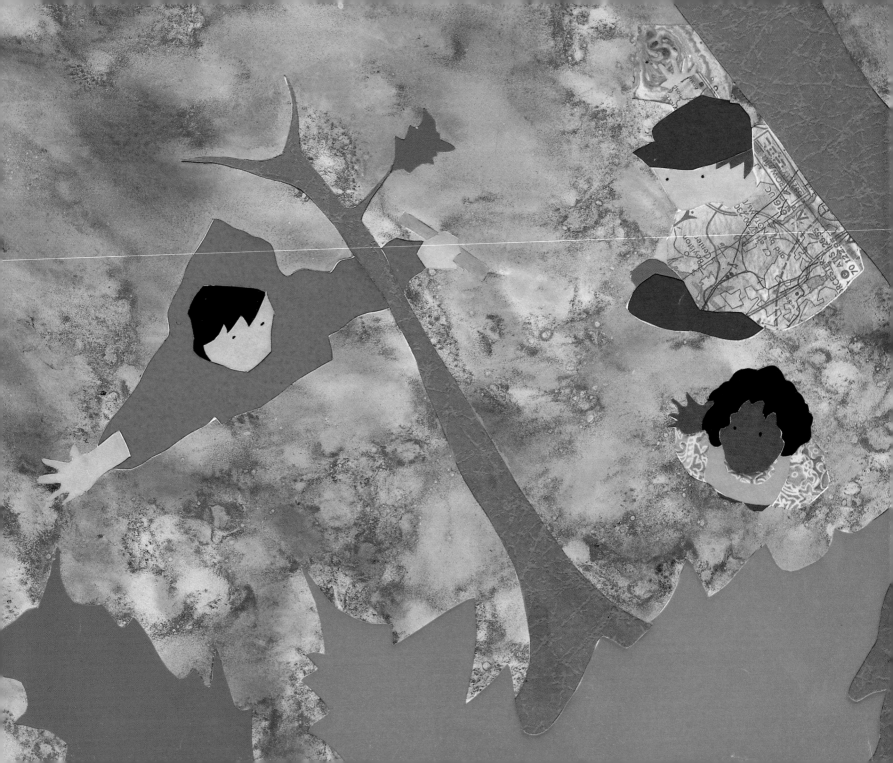

They begin to catch
in the shuddery air,
softly falling,
slowly turning,
like a wind ballet.

Then faster and faster!

Diving and dropping,

orange and brown heap up on the ground.

Krish-krash! Ka-rak!

We sciff and scuff the colors up,

snatching the crackly runaway leaves
as they spin ahead of us.

Sha-shoo! Ska-tat!
We jump through the twig-snappy piles
and crunch up a smell like spicy toast
while the acorns roll underfoot.

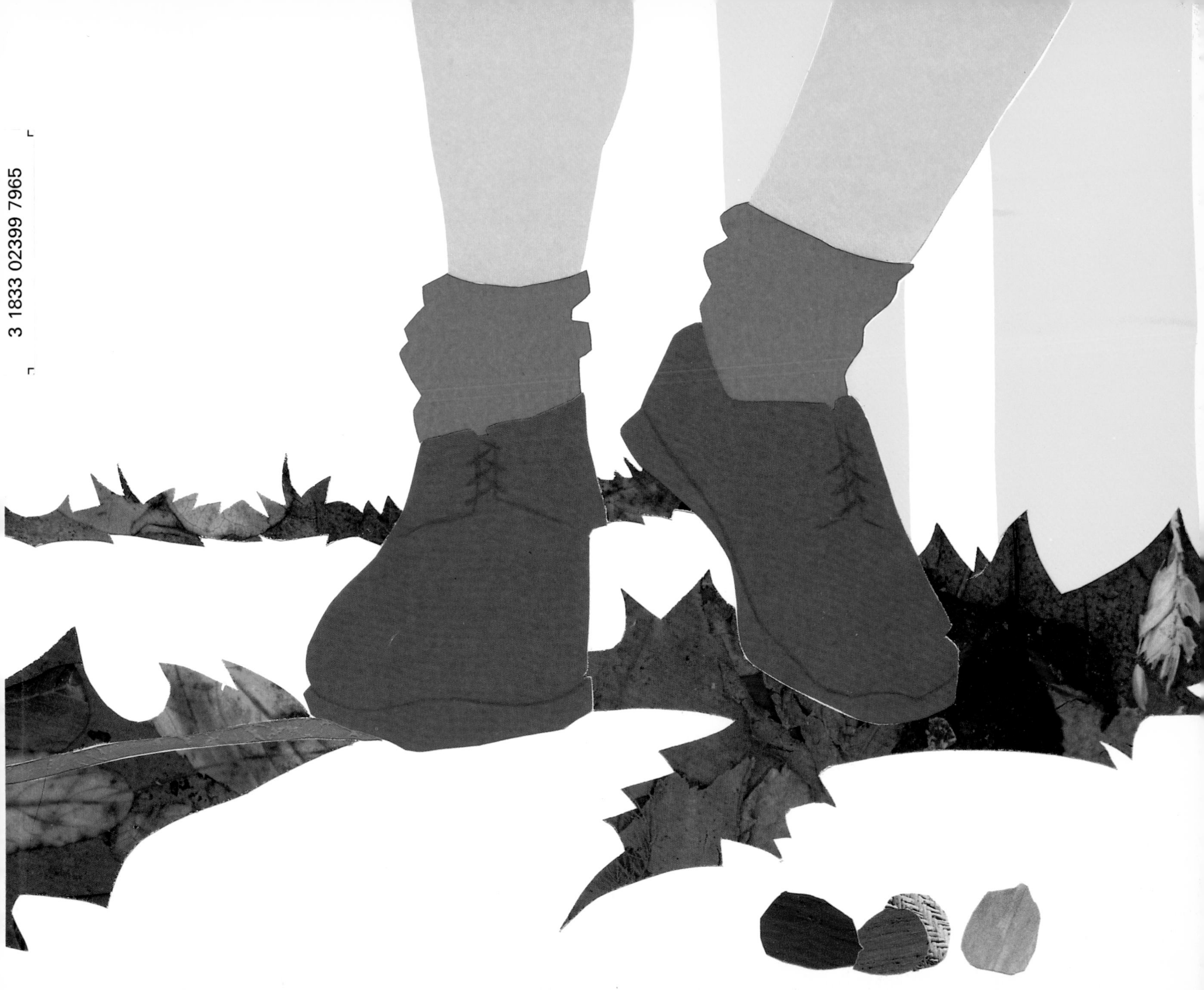

Faster and FASTER! We race on the scrunch:

Krish-krash! Ka-rak! Sha-shoo! Ska-tat!

Out past the fence, now slower and slower…
until we reach the leaf mountains
ready for us to climb.

Deeper and DEEPER and **DEEPER** we jump
into the mountains. And all around our ears we hear:
Krish-krash! Ka-rak! Sha-shoo! Ska-tat!

The leaves are scratchy,
spilling over us as we barrel in.

We sort them by color
and rake them in rows
to look like a garden.

At our harvest, our eyelids squeeze tight-shut!

We throw big handfuls in the air:

Krish-krash! Ka-rak! Sha-shoo! Ska-tat!
They tickle us fluttering down.

The leaves stick as they fall,
to our sweaters and pants.
We are monsters with tails:

Krish-krash! Ka-ROAR! Sha-shoo ska-tat!
We scare each other until our tails fall off.

We stop to make magic dust

by grinding the leaves into a fine, fiery powder.

Sh-kah sh-kah…like the leaves, it blows away.

We sit in the itchy-gold yellowness
and listen as the crashed-down mountains
skitter off in the wind:
Shshsh…kah  Shshsh…kah  Shshsh…

The shadows grow long as we softly call:

Good-bye, Krish-krash Ka-rak…

Good-bye, Sha-shoo Ska-tat.

But before we go,
we carefully save
the brightest leaves of all.